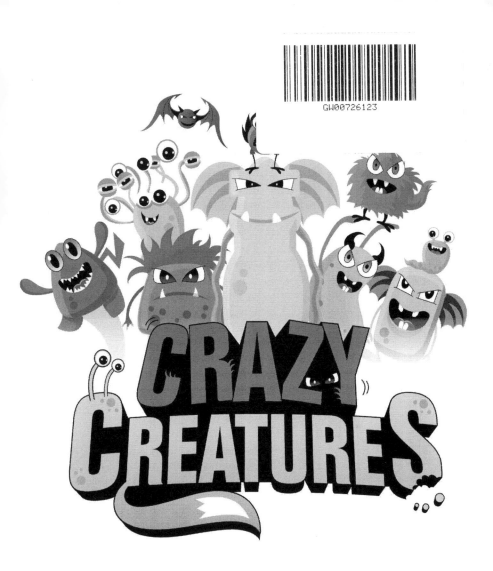

CRAZY CREATURES

WONDERFUL WRITERS

Edited By Lynsey Evans

First published in Great Britain in 2024 by:

Young Writers
Remus House
Coltsfoot Drive
Peterborough
PE2 9BF
Telephone: 01733 890066
Website: www.youngwriters.co.uk

FOREWORD

Welcome Reader!

Are you ready to discover weird and wonderful creatures that you'd never even dreamed of?

For Young Writers' latest competition we asked primary school pupils to create a creature of their own invention, and then write a mini saga about it - a hard task! However, they rose to the challenge magnificently and the result is this fantastic collection full of creepy critters and bizarre beasts!

Here at Young Writers our aim is to encourage creativity in children and to inspire a love of the written word, so it's great to get such an amazing response, with some absolutely fantastic stories.

Not only have these young authors created imaginative and inventive creatures, they've also crafted wonderful tales to showcase their creations. These stories are brimming with inspiration and cover a wide range of themes and emotions - from fun to fear and back again!

I'd like to congratulate all the young authors in this anthology, I hope this inspires them to continue with their creative writing.

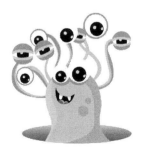

CONTENTS

Ethan Russell (9)	69
Elena Bullock (9)	70
Louie Tyler (10)	71
Evie-Rose Harley (9)	72
Jaiden Pearson (10)	73
Freddie O'Neil (10)	74
Darcie Marlow (10)	75
Amelia Sayers (10)	76
Charlie Lakin (9)	77

St Anne's Catholic Primary School, Leyland

Caitlin Taylor (10)	78
Emma Firth	79
James Hopkins (9)	80
Max Burgess (9)	81
Kian Robinson	82
Emily Miskolczi (10)	83
Tia Price (9)	84
Elliot Barnes (10)	85
Sophie Moss (9)	86
Kian Dickinson (10)	87
Noah Larkin (9)	88
Daisy-Mae Ball (10)	89
Nadia Matuszny (10)	90
Rory Winder (10)	91

The Batt CE Primary School, Witney

Daniel Fares (8)	92
Sophie Wakefield (8)	93
Ray Garbrah (7)	94
Zach Wyatt (8)	95
Livvi Green (8)	96
Mollie Armson (8)	97

Waringstown Primary School, Waringstown

Jasper Clarke (10)	98
Penny Hanna (10)	99
Alexander Buchanan (10)	100

Maisie Harrison (10)	101
Joshua Hutchinson (10)	102
Phoebe Armstrong (8)	103
Ella Bushe (10)	104
Aimee May Freeburn (9)	105
Erin Peacocke (8)	106
Elise Liggett (9)	107
Edward Cassells (9)	108
Noah Budde (10)	109
Tiffany Brown (8)	110
Ella Owens (9)	111
Ezra Gault (10)	112
Isaac Wethers (9)	113
Joshua Wylie (10)	114
Harley Hughes (8)	115
Molly Lockhart (10)	116
Chloe Cunningham (10)	117
Elisabeth Smyth (10)	118
Dinah Glendinning (9)	119
Adam Coffey (9)	120
Noah Chestnutt (10)	121
Micah Parks (9)	122
Jake Robinson (9)	123
Noah McIlwaine (9)	124
Aimee McCullough (8)	125
Lucy Ball (9)	126
Noah McAdam (9)	127
Amelia Armstrong (10)	128
Ben Whittaker (9)	129
Alfie Davidson (8)	130
Emily Derby (9)	131
Lucas Thompson (10)	132
Lily-Anna Hutchinson (9)	133
Clara Little (9)	134
Sophie Bailey (8)	135
Isaac White (10)	136
Jessica Riddle (9)	137
Scarlett Thompson (8)	138
Poppy Thompson (10)	139
Jamie Thornbury (9)	140
William Massey (10)	141
Josiah Martin (10)	142
Maisie Adair (9)	143

Luke Hunter (9)	144
Leah Parker (9)	145
Esme Magowan-Wilton (9)	146
Brandon Elliott (9)	147
Daniel Hamill (10)	148
Annie McCallum (10)	149
James Grant (9)	150
Nina Kraicova (9)	151
Eva Morrow (10)	152
Archie McCullough (9)	153
Rhys Burns (10)	154
Oliver Wright (10)	155
Zachary McGrath (9)	156
Jacob Irwin (10)	157
Sarah Fitzpatrick (10)	158
Alexandra Emo (10)	159
Amber Dawson (8)	160
Dawid Pawlowski (10)	161
Kayla Brooks (9)	162
Blake Cooper (10)	163
Lauren Orr (8)	164
Thomas Alexander (10)	165
Konstancja Halaburda (10)	166
Sebastian McAllister (9)	167
Gracie-May Gore (9)	168

Woolton Primary School, Woolton

Ben Harris (10)	169
Isla Blu Geraghty (11)	170
Grace Reid (11)	171
Eben Price (11)	172
Bobbi-Mai Keating (10)	173
Beth Palmer (10)	174
Yizhi Qi (10)	175
Ella Dyce (11)	176

THE STORIES

Bobby's Favourite Day Ever

"Bobby, the Easter bunny is real!"

"I don't believe! Prove!"

This is Bobby's first Easter. His sister wants to show him the Easter bunny, but he doesn't believe her. She tries all day setting up traps and cameras, but nothing! "I-idea! Me, no sleep! I stay to see the bunny."

"Yes, Bobby!"

Ten hours later... "Hi, Bobby, I've got a very special gift for you."

"It's a notepad and pens! I've always wanted these!"

The next day, he drew a picture of his family.

"Aww, thank you, Bobby! It's beautiful!" From that day on, he drew everything on his notepad of family.

Libbie Lagden (9)
Hilldene Primary School, Romford

Crazy Talent Show Goes Wrong!

"Welcome to the talent show. Up first the act is Shadow, he can scare humans, evil and other monsters."

"Aah!"

"Sorry."

"Thanks, next, Poo Haria can juggle five eyes. That is a lot."

Alert, alert, fire!

"Evacuate, everyone, quick!"

One hour later...

False alert! Oh no...

"Pigtales time!"

"*Nooo!*"

"Okay, we have something weird. A cook..."

One hour later...

Winner time.

"What about Axe? He has an axe and kills your pencil! Stay safe from him, pencils. Okay... Fire! Everyone, run!"

"My bag!"
"My homework!"
"My desk!"
Everything broke.
"Wait, once I was seven years old..."
"Okay, that's it, Poo Haria's won."
"What?"
"Congratulations."

Jeyda Huseyin (8)
Hilldene Primary School, Romford

Blobby's Great Adventure!

Once upon a time, there lived a slime called Blobby. He was sad because he had no friends. So, Blobby travelled the world, trying to find a friend. He met lots of animals and creatures, big and small. But just couldn't find the right friend. When he checked the last place in the world, he thought there was no one there, then he saw a house. He knocked on the door, there was a slime. A pink slime. Blobby said, "Hello, what's your name?" "My name is Pinky," said the pink slime. "Mine is Blobby."
A few years later, they got married and had kids. They lived happily ever after.

Lily Moxham (8)
Hilldene Primary School, Romford

Heradina And The Flying Monster Academy

Welcome to Flying Monster Academy.
This is where monsters learn how to fly.
This is Heradina. She's probably the best. "Hey, Sofie! I made a bracelet for you. I made it all by myself. I hope you really like it, Sofie!" Heradina was walking in the academy when she saw someone stuck. Maybe the hairy, one-eyed, blue monster.
"Hey, let me help you," and at this moment, the monster jumped out.
"Heradina! It was a joke!"
"Haha," Heradina laughed heartily.
The next day, everybody was very happy. They grabbed their hands and went to find brand-new adventures.

Mia Bareikis (8)
Hilldene Primary School, Romford

5

Batchocolate Vs Aquacandyland Battle

Bataculla was the Queen of Batchocolate. She had an army of four-eyed and two-legged flying spiders that could eat things 200 times their size. Batchocolate was under attack from the army of Aquacandyland. The king had sent an army of his snapping speedy giant crocodiles to battle for power. There was an epic battle with a lot of snapping, chewing, biting and screaming.

Bataculla had had enough.

He screamed at the top of his lungs, "*Stooooop*, no more fighting."

The queen shouted back, "Let's get married and rule both lands and become the most powerful king and queen to rule."

Arveen Passi (7)
Hilldene Primary School, Romford

The Monster Who Finds Friends

One day, a monster named Furrymespotace had no friends, so he decided to fly across space. He flew to Mars and found a monster called Bob. Furrymespotface asked, "Can we be friends?"

"No, thank you!" Bob shouted, so Furrymespotface flew to Venus, went into a cave and found a monster named Lilly.

Furrymespotface asked, "Can we be friends?"

Lilly said, "Only if you give me a hundred pounds."

"I have nine hundred and ninety-nine thousand pounds!" said Furrymespotface.

Lilly said, "Okay, that's enough. Let's be friends."

Jethro Bangali (8)
Hilldene Primary School, Romford

The Magic Pencil

Amelia and Frank went to the market to buy a pencil.

Frank saw a pencil he liked, so he asked Amelia, "Can I buy this pencil?"

Amelia said, "Sure, dear."

They bought it. Then, Amelia suggested that Frank use the pencil very carefully. Frank drew an apple and slept. Then, the apple turned alive. Frank told Amelia about the magic pencil. Amelia suggested to Frank that he use the pencil to help poor people. So they gave us a blessing and they felt happy that this was the best use of the magic. Frank used the pencil to help others. The moral of the story is to help others.

Aashita Jain (7)
Hilldene Primary School, Romford

Lamizo And The Girl

Once upon a time, there was a monster called Lamizo and a girl called Fiona. Then, one day, Fiona was in the park when she saw a monster and Fiona froze because she got scared.
Lamizo said, "Don't be scared!"
Fiona said, "Oh, I didn't mean to make you sad."
Lamizo smiled, "Do you want to be friends?"
Fiona just stood there and suddenly said, "Yes!"
They began to play in the park. Fiona went on the swing, and Lamizo went on the slide. After that, they got some ice cream. Lamizo got strawberry ice cream and Fiona got chocolate.

Lois Graves (8)
Hilldene Primary School, Romford

9

The Long-Lost Monster

Mr. Fiercefighter was in his rocket travelling towards Mars. He got distracted by a phone call. Once he had finished talking, he looked out of the window and *boom!* He crashed. When he looked, he saw blue things everywhere.

"Mars isn't blue," he said.

"Oh no, I've landed on Earth."

He lost his rocket because it had crashed and he used his wings to get to a place in England.

"How did I get here?" he wondered.

Then, he remembered that he had wings. He flew back up to the moon. Mr Fiercefighter used his fire to kill his enemy.

Sudarshan Singh (8)
Hilldene Primary School, Romford

The Stick Snake

Once, there was a snake and an odd one, I suppose. It had fangs, wings and fire at the tip of its tail. This mysterious creature is named Snake-A-La-Boo. Snake-A-La-Boo was out slithering in the forest until he came across a school, a big one! He wondered, *should I go in or not? Yes!* He went in right when it was playtime. The same kids noticed him and stopped playing football.
"What's this? A stick!"
"I saw it move!" said one of the kids.
Snake-A-La-Boo was worried and flew off.
"Aah, why is this stick flying? It is living!"

Mia Sindila (10)
Hilldene Primary School, Romford

Mimi's Big Win!

Once there was a monster called Mimi. She was very small. One day she entered a competition. It was an athletic competition. The winner got a crown. Mimi's brother also entered. She did a cartwheel, he did a backflip. When she did her cartwheel the crowd went wild. When her brother went they only clapped. It was tough, there were lots of entries. The winner was announced. The judge said, "Drum roll please."
It was Mimi! When she looked at her brother he was crying. Mimi hugged her brother. "Size doesn't matter. Being short means you're strong too."

Chloe Redgrove (10)
Hilldene Primary School, Romford

Forbidden Forest Escape

Late one eerie evening, Killer Tooth Rabbit heard Feelix Fox shouting, "I'm coming to get you." Killer Tooth Rabbit started to run super-fast through the spooky forbidden forest. Suddenly, he was stopped by Sam, the scary spider and his army of eight-legged friends.

"Oh, no! What am I going to do? Feelix is too close." Killer Tooth Rabbit charged through the legs of the spiders and knocked Sam to the ground. "Yes! I did it! I beat the spiders and made it back home safely." Feelix Fox stood no chance. Killer Tooth Rabbit was just too quick.

Bella Smith (7)
Hilldene Primary School, Romford

Problem Solving

Once upon a time, there was a creature called Mushy. Mushy was a creature who helped people with problems. One time Mushy helped someone who was getting bullied every single day. But Mushy tried to help that person but Mushy couldn't. So Mushy had to ignore it, but he was desperate. So he faced his fears and went up to the bully like a boss.

Mushy said, "Stop! Leave him alone!"

Then the bully got scared and left. So Mushy helped the guy and he was pleased.

Then the guy said, "Let's be friends."

And Mushy said, "Sure."

Sonia Balde (10)
Hilldene Primary School, Romford

The Shadow Shimmer

Down in the deep sea where it's really dark, there's this creature called The Shadow Shimmer. It's like a mix of bright lights and scary shadows all rolled into one. Imagine a big glowing jellyfish with wiggly eyes, sharp teeth and long, wavy arms that seem to reach you. People say it's got secrets about the oceans, but others warn it might eat you up. Still, some brave folks can't resist checking it out. As they approach, hearts pounding with anticipation, they remind themselves: sometimes, the greatest discoveries are found in the most unlikely places.

Anaya Khakwani (8)
Hilldene Primary School, Romford

Mr Sneaky-Spider

Once, in a world with lots of spiders, everyone was scared of them. They killed all of the tiny, small spiders.

Then all of a sudden there was a massive spider that everyone hated.

"Look out!" the humans shouted out. "The massive spider's coming!"

His talent was to sneak into cups and blend in so no one would know when they drank the tea. There was only a weird, tingly strange feeling in their mouth, crawling around and then biting their tongue.

Then they fished him out of their mouths and he crawled out onto everyone's face!

Tanyel Dellaloglu (11)
Hilldene Primary School, Romford

A Cranham's Life

A meteor crashed into Earth. The Cranham awoke and heard it crash with a mighty bang which demolished the whole Earth. A new species arrived on the destroyed Earth but couldn't survive due to the enemy of the Cranham, the Sackive! Cranham liked to eat toxic waste, hot red lava and molten rock once cooled. The Sackive liked to eat anything, including Cranham! Cranham and Sackive fought for many years, which rolled into decades, each side had many losses. Cranham was outnumbered by ten to one but due to smart planning, the Cranham managed to overcome the Sackive and win.

Tank Banham (8)
Hilldene Primary School, Romford

The Mean Sisters

Once upon a time, there was a girl called Scary Lary. She came from Doodoo Land.

One day, when she was looking for her earrings, her mum said, "Here! And pack your things. We're leaving!" They left and went to Pollyester Land. Five days later, she started school and became a prankster. One day, she pranked the mean sisters, Mean Maya, Mean Maddy and Mean Maddison. Then she became a mean sister, so there were four mean sisters, Mean Maya, Mean Maddy, Mean Maddison and Mean Scary Lary. She was the newest sister in the mean sisters and she was cooler.

Anna Coseriu (8)
Hilldene Primary School, Romford

Never Be Ashamed Of What You Do

One day, this girl called Brook was really popular but one day she lost it. She did a big burp and she also tripped over in front of her crush. As the bell rang, it was time for home and Brook cried, but then, this creature came to her and said, "Don't be embarrassed. Do what is comfortable for you."
The creature gave her a hug and the other creature, Fang said, "Don't be ashamed of who you are."
The next day Brook dropped all the mean words about her out of her zone and remembered what the creatures said. Don't worry.

Mollie Skinner (10)
Hilldene Primary School, Romford

19

Spotzo Great Adventurer

Spotzo, a monster from Planet Monstropolis enjoyed making fellow monsters laugh. One day a spaceship crashed in Spotzo's garden. Inside was a human called Alex. Alex and Spotzo were scared of each other at first, but then they became friends. Alex was upset because his ship was broken, Spotzo cheered Alex up by making him laugh and then helped him fix his ship. Once it was fixed, Spotzo and Alex hugged and said goodbye. Alex flew into space with a happy smile, Spotzo smiled and waved knowing they would always be friends no matter how far they lived away.

Isabelle Rhodes (10)
Hilldene Primary School, Romford

Stacy And Calt

There was a seven-year-old girl called Stacy, worried because of toothache. A monster lived under her bed, who was small, fluffy and named 'Calt' by Stacy. He came from space and was able to extend his arms and sharpen his claws as he wished. Calt had no enemies because he was not a scary creature who frightened children just for fun. However, Calt decided to help Stacy relieve her toothache. He extended his arms and sharpened claws, gently wiggled the affected tooth and took it off with no pain. Stacy and Calt became very happy and playful friends.

Jaanavi Sugith (7)
Hilldene Primary School, Romford

Lost Pearls!

She was a magical mermaid who swam across the seas, hidden away in the deep ocean. Her name was Queen Pearl, but her perfect life would soon be filled with worry.

One quiet day, as Pearl was swimming, she was stopped by a large net.

Quickly, she was taken up towards the sky, trapped with crabs, fish and lobsters.

Then as she reached the fresh air, she saw the humans. They looked scared to see her, but happy to see the powerful, shining, pearl crown on Pearl's head.

How much is this worth? they thought and took it from her.

Maisie Allen (8)
Hilldene Primary School, Romford

The Battle Begins

Exeus entered his ship and typed where he wanted to go.

"To Planet Blob," he said.

As he entered Planet Blob he wondered if the Blob Raiders would be there. He gently stepped out of the ship. Suddenly, the Blob Raiders attacked him and his army (a monkey). They took him away and captured him and that's when he found out that he had stretchy legs. He used his stretchy legs to get out of there and defeat the Blob Raiders. *Bang! Boom!* He took them all down. Then he went back to his ship and flew to another big adventure.

Joshua Child (10)
Hilldene Primary School, Romford

The Booger Man

In the heart of the murky bog, where whispers danced with mist, lived the Booger Man. With skin like swamp moss and eyes that glowed with an otherworldly light, he was the keeper of secrets and the guardian of the marsh. Some said that he was a lost soul, cursed to wander the wetland for eternity. Others whispered of his ability to shape-shift into any creature in the night. But one thing remained certain - those who dared to trespass in his domain never returned. And so, the legend of the Booger Man grew, haunting the minds of all who dared venture.

Ryshana Haryshan (9)

Hilldene Primary School, Romford

Sports Room Monster Story

In the sports room was a basketball with a mouth and connected to it were two whistles, a tennis racket arm and two hockey stick legs. But the monster found out one of his arms was missing, so he just made it out of some balls and a glove. Once, it was a sports club and someone saw him trying to escape back to the sports room, but one of the kids, called Charlie, said, "Come out of the shadows."
So the monster did. Even though Charlie was shocked, he said, "We can play together."
And so the monster had friends.

Jake Smith (11)
Hilldene Primary School, Romford

25

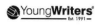

All About My Crazy Creature

He runs away, changes colour and hunts people. They both can change anything that they want to, hunt food and drink from rivers. They drink Sprite and Fanta and steal things from all of the shops. Their favourite food is only burgers, and their favourite sweets are lollipops, milkshakes and gummies and their favourite drinks are cola, Sprite and Fanta. Their friends are Dama and Lama and their favourite shop is Tesco. Their favourite restaurant is McDonald's and the second is Burget King, and their favourite countries are Spain and France.

Patrick Albu (8)

Hilldene Primary School, Romford

The Cyclops, The Alien Monster

Out of this world, there was an alien named the Cyclops Monster. The Cyclops could change into any shape. He had no enemies from his planet. The alien was sent to Earth and his spaceship broke down and he had the special ability that he could change into any shape he wanted, like a triangle or a circle, or even a table. He saw a little girl named Emily and he followed her. He stayed in Emily's house and no one knew about it. One day, Emily heard a sound in the sitting room and she saw the Cyclops alien and she was impressed by his skills.

Lucy Odzoemenam (11)

Hilldene Primary School, Romford

Fear! Disappear!

Miley was getting ready for bed as in the morning she was starting a new school. Miley was nervous so she closed her eyes and made a wish. All of a sudden, a bright, white light and a pink, fluffy monster with three eyes appeared.

"Nervous?" said the monster. "Give me a squeeze and your fear will ease."

Miley was scared but she did as it said. She then felt relaxed and tucked herself in bed. She fell asleep quickly and with a cheer the monster said, "My name is the Bleep and my job here is complete."

Olivia Erwood (10)
Hilldene Primary School, Romford

Slimy Changes The Bully!

There was this slime named Slimy; when he was in school, he got bullied by the slime destroyer. Then, it all changed because of Slimy. Slimy talked to the bully to convince him to stop bullying Slimes, but that didn't work. So, Slimy morphed into someone similar. Then, they noticed each other and started to chat. Slimy was himself and the bully started to warm up to him. He told Slimy some secrets. Slimy was loyal and didn't tell anyone. The bully found out it was Slimy, but he turned out to like him, so they became best friends.

Hope Gater (10)
Hilldene Primary School, Romford

James And The Ocean

One time, James was driving down the highway when a car appeared beside him. He asked if he wanted to race, so he agreed. They raced down the highway when they heard a beeping. James didn't think much of it, but he realised he had run out of fuel. The car disappeared and an object appeared. He saw a mysterious object that started appearing and realised it was a submarine. He got in and it teleported to the ocean. He went down and saw coral and fish. It went super fast when he heard beeping. James woke up and it was all a dream.

David Sava

Hilldene Primary School, Romford

Giggling In The Shadows

Far away in a land of cats called Cattopia, lived a mischievous and giggly cat, Giggly Gabby. Gabby loved to joke and play tricks on people, she was also able to cheer them up! Gabby had one enemy, Grumpy Green. He was unhappy all the time and they used to fight a lot. Although this happened often, Gabby didn't care and still stayed all giggly and happy. Gabby enjoyed eating if she ever felt sad, it made it go away! You could never really see her feeling down and she probably won't really be! Gabby will always be with you!

Maya Barbu (10)
Hilldene Primary School, Romford

The Fierce Friendship

One day, a girl and her conservationist dad took a trip to the Amazon rainforest. Ella decided she wanted to explore, so she wandered off. While Ella was exploring, she found a bird's nest close to the ground. In the nest, she saw a strange-looking leopard. It had wings! Suddenly, it flew up and out of the nest and did a loop-the-loop. All of a sudden, Ella heard a voice and she didn't know where it was coming from. Then, she realised it was the leopard. They started to chat and became best friends. Ella named her Leila.

Rosie McKenzie (10)
Hilldene Primary School, Romford

Crazyland Cup

It was the final of the Crazyland Cup. Isobel's team would be playing and they had to win. Isobel was the goalie. Everyone said there was something about her which made her special. At half-time, the score was 0-0. The second half started. Isobel seemed different. She was in goal one minute, then at the other end trying to score the next. Isobel had a secret power. She could run at the speed of light. At the final whistle, the score was 3-0 and Isobel's team had won without anyone realising who had even scored the goals.

Alfie Smith (8)
Hilldene Primary School, Romford

The Adventures Of Boogie In Boogie Vs Mr Glue

One beautiful morning, Boogie and his friends were having a picnic at the park. Suddenly, Mr Glue showed up! Mr Glue said he would make a deal with Boogie.

"Let's have a fight. If you win, then I go to jail. And if I win, I get to glue the city!"

So Boogie and Mr Glue had a big fight. Boogie was throwing snot balls while Mr Glue was trying to glue Boogie. Boogie frantically dodged glue and as for Mr Glue? Well, he could not really dodge. Finally, the battle ended, Boogie had won. So Mr Glue went to jail!

Vasile Basarab (8)
Hilldene Primary School, Romford

Shahapp Overpowered Ability!

Citizens from Planet Pluto are at war with soldiers from Eris Planet. Prince Shahapp from Planet Pluto, with two faces, one happy and one sad, stretchy long ears, has the ability to shoot fireballs when he is grumpy.

Shahapp was captured by the Eris soldiers because of his ability to shoot fireballs as hot as the sun. They wanted to use these fireballs to make this overpowerful laser gun to destroy Pluto. Shahapp was rescued by his father's spacecraft. Prince Shahapp came back excited and lived happily on planet Pluto.

Lucas Marios Simion (7)

Hilldene Primary School, Romford

Astro The Fantastic Alien

Once upon a time, there was an alien named Astro. First, he was wondering what was on Earth. So he launched himself onto Earth and when he got there he could see grass and buildings. After that, it turned morning and he saw a little bot. Astro hid, but he was found and soon his enemy came, the evil but clever Invisible Cyclops. Urgently he wanted to defeat Astro but Astro won. Happily, he launched himself back into space and when he got home he relaxed. Before long he heard a knock at the door, it was his friends celebrating.

Luca Palimaru (8)
Hilldene Primary School, Romford

The Cold, Dark Night

One night it was cold and dark. Dancey was walking in the streets. He saw Shortey, his enemy. Dancey did his ice dance and Shortey froze. Next week Shortey was now giant and Dancey was scared. Then Dancey and Shortey were friends. Then they found a new enemy, Yeti.
Two days later Dancey and Shortey saw Yeti at 6pm. Dancey did his ice dance but Yeti did not freeze. Yeti hit Shorty, then Shorty kicked Yeti, he fell but was fine.
Yeti said, "Stop. Why are we fighting? We will get hurt. Let's stop. Okay?"

Daniel Kazakevicius (8)
Hilldene Primary School, Romford

The Revenge Seeker And Dog

Miss Spooky Ghost went to walk her dog. She was crossing the road and a car was speeding. The car crashed into her. The dog got minor injuries and Miss Spooky Ghost was taken to the hospital. After doing checks on her, the doctors declared her dead. The dog understood what the doctors were saying and started to cry. Miss Spooky Ghost went to heaven and turned into a ghost. She came back to haunt her killer. Her dog had felt her presence back on Earth and started to cry again. Miss Spooky found her killer and got her revenge.

Sukhwinder Kaur (10)
Hilldene Primary School, Romford

Ask And You Shall Receive

One day, an octopus-looking creature was far, far away from shore, from his family! So, he searched and searched and still no luck. He kept on searching, but no luck still. He then started to cry as there was no luck for him. He started to go to sleep and dreamed, *what if somebody came to get me back to my family?* He then remembered he had to pray for someone to get him, so that's what he did. He prayed and prayed, "God, if you bring me someone to help me, I'll pay you back!" And someone came.

Mihnea Bojoran (9)
Hilldene Primary School, Romford

The Mystical Zog

Zog is a wild tricky creature from Forest Zalandra. Zog has bright fur, twisted horns and leafy wings. It can change into any creature it wants, which helps it hide. Zog is good at copying animals to trick its enemies. Zog's biggest enemy is Zada, a smart witch who wants to steal Zog's magic. When Zog goes on a big adventure to find a special thing that can give unlimited power, Zog faces lots of problems and meets new friends on the way. Zog stops Zada's bad plans, saving Zalandria and becoming a big hero.

Maria Ciugureanu (9)
Hilldene Primary School, Romford

The Mr Floppy Longhand's Life

On the day he was born, his arms were so long! He was born on a spaceship.

He felt excited about growing up, so he danced.

Once he was ready to go to school, he saw so many short-handed people! Outrageous! So he left. Every time he saw a short-handed person, he got his fangs out and flew. He became so fierce! He flew until he calmed down.

One day, he met a beautiful woman with long hands. It was love at first sight, so he asked for her to marry him. She said - yes!

They lived happily together.

Barbora Kvietkus (10)
Hilldene Primary School, Romford

Escape The Swamp

One mysterious morning there was a monster, his name was Groosy Gooly and he heard creepy cries coming from the deep, dark forest. He found a young boy stuck in a sticky swamp, filled with his arch enemies, Colby Cobra and his army of snakes. Groosy Gooly flipped around the swamp for a rope. He threw the rope high in the trees where Maurice the monkey tied it. Groosy Gooly flew across and saved the terrified boy from the swamp and snakes.

"Thank you," said Edward.

Then they became best friends.

Blayke Smith (7)

Hilldene Primary School, Romford

Dilly And Her Enemies

One day, a girl called Dilly was born. Her childhood was bad; kids bullied her, but her brother protected her. One day, she wanted to be a hero and she gave food to the poor and donated to charity. One day, she met her enemy, the Devil. One time, the Devil called Hameus on Dilly, but she did not care at all. One day, the Devil tried to defeat her, but Dilly was too weak. Suddenly, her family came and they defeated the Devil. Dilly's dream came true and she was the Queen and the Devil was never seen again.

Sofia Gurguri Dzatdojeva (8)
Hilldene Primary School, Romford

The Rainbow Turtle

Once upon a time, there lived a rainbow turtle with a rainbow shell and a shimmering pink horn. She lived in London's pet store called Adopt Me. All the other turtles bullied her because of her horn. But one day, that all changed; she escaped and went to the ocean and travelled to Candy Land. There, she made it rain candy and made a boat and met some candy pets, some candy cats and dogs and chocolate bunnies and hamsters. Then, the turtle made it rain gingerbread and made a house for them to enjoy.

Amelia Whitehurst (8)
Hilldene Primary School, Romford

Lovely Leila

Leila, a lovely little girl with a heart of gold, was in danger. Malcom Misfortune had chosen Leila as his next target, due to the joy she gave to others. Lucifer Luck was in another country when he sensed that his brother was up to no good again and flew off quickly. Meanwhile, Malcom had caused Leila to fall and drop her money, which flew far away. Suddenly, the money came back towards Leila. It was Lucifer! But Leila couldn't see Lucifer. Malcom smirked at his brother before running off again.

Leila Williams (9)
Hilldene Primary School, Romford

Crazy

One day, Gooie Googily saw Dark Skull and with his hoe, he cut his eyes off but out of nowhere, he saw a little kid with suction cups at the bottom of his feet. He spat the eyes back at Dark Skull. He was about to pass out and he died. Gooie Googily's eyes were so overwhelmed the war was over, no more fighting. He returned back to his eye family. *Dark Skull has returned Gooie Googily's eyes*, he heard in his head, but he thought he was crazy, but Dark Skull was outside of the window.

Joey Cross (10)
Hilldene Primary School, Romford

The Monster And Hermen!

Once upon a time, there lived a monster named Friendly. He was very hairy and had one eye. He could see people very well except one, a girl, who was bad because she was a Hemen monster. He didn't like Hemens. She was very kind, but she didn't trust him. In the afternoon, they both learned to like each other. They played games and were best friends forever. At the end of the day, they both told the teacher and the teacher told them now they are the best of friends. They live happily together.

Robyn Senior (7)
Hilldene Primary School, Romford

YoungWriters
Est. 1991

The Slurping Mobile

One day, a little creature found itself on a planet called Klyntar. It was very fun in Klyntar, slurping soup and torturing people with her venom tongue. She walked around the city, looking for fun until she saw her enemy, Little Long Legs. They talked and talked for ages and became best villain friends forever. They ganged up on people endlessly. They met up and went to the cheese shop, stole a stack of fresh yellow junk and ate it all in one bite. Little Long Legs confessed to Slurping Mobile.

Yvette Odei (9)
Hilldene Primary School, Romford

Fuzzyba's Story

Once upon a time, there was a little egg that hatched. A human came up to it like it was an ordinary egg and they left it like it was nothing, which made her upset. So she took care of herself all day. But as she grew older, her skills improved so much that she grew her own wings. She was so happy to fly and it was the best skill she ever had. She was the best monster ever. But the human from last time wanted her, but she said no. That's why you shouldn't judge a book by its cover.

Gabriela Tudor (11)
Hilldene Primary School, Romford

Curl

In your very classroom, there is this blue fuzzy creature that hides in the corner of the classroom, so whenever Curl rolls around he has fun. When you're in class you unexpectedly hear an odd sound. A fun fact about Curl is that he had to travel from the Curl Galaxy to ours. He had to come to his one because he just can't learn, so to make the noises he curls up and rolls through your classroom floors and nobody knows where, who or what galaxy he will be forced to go to for education.

Alessandra Lungu (9)
Hilldene Primary School, Romford

The Earth Mission

One day on Planet Snotabog a reporter gave Ogabog a mission to head down to the human world to see what a human week is like. The day arrived for him to complete his mission, so he headed to the reporter and told him he was leaving. He flew down and when he arrived it was night so he slept. When he awoke he met a girl named Abigail and she told and showed him all the wonders of Earth. As time flew by, Ogabog had to leave, he said goodbye and went to tell the reporter and they praised him.

Poppy Schooling (9)
Hilldene Primary School, Romford

The Monster Under My Bed

Once upon a time, a person called Jape woke up and didn't find his phone. He looked under his bed and saw there were creatures eating his phone. He woke up everyone and still didn't find anything. He looked for his iPad - gone. His laptop was nowhere to be seen and he was annoyed. He tried to buy a new one, but they were gone. He tried and tried but still couldn't buy it because he was losing money and they kept eating, so he tried to keep it in a secret place but still, gone.

Dylan Skinner (7)
Hilldene Primary School, Romford

The Easter Monster

There was a monster who was called Hoppy. He didn't have many friends because he got bullied. Hoppy was a special monster, but no one noticed that he saved Easter.

Let me explain why Hoppy was a big fan of Easter. Every year he caught the Easter bunny. Hoppy knew something was wrong. So he got all his chocolate eggs from his kitchen and jumped from house to house hiding them and that was how he saved Easter, no one knew.

The next year, the Easter Bunny thankfully came.

Riley Luxford (10)
Hilldene Primary School, Romford

Stitch And His Best Friend

There was a boy named Stitch. He went to Creature School and on his first day, he got a best friend. They never left each other and always helped each other. On the next day, Stitch found out his best friend's name was Zac. They had a sleepover the next day.

They were best friends for life. At the sleepover, they had a pillow fight. Zac had a sleepover at Stitch's house and they always sat next to each other every day at lunch. Stitch and Zac were best friends forever.

Bella Marshall (8)

Hilldene Primary School, Romford

The Dare

I was walking to the haunted house I was dared to go to for £500. Going into the house, I felt a chill going down my spine. The door of the haunted house opened at 3am, 6am and 9am. The house looked strangely familiar, but I ignored that. I went to the toilet and when I turned the tap on, blood came out. I let out a blood-curdling scream before sprinting out of the bathroom. I went downstairs and dozed off and when I woke up, the door was open.
Finally, it was 9am.

Amna Bilal (10)
Hilldene Primary School, Romford

The Lonely Dog

It all started this week. I ate as usual until everything changed. My owner got another dog! His name was Freddy. Freddy was a posh dog and he didn't like anything. He hated living in our manky, old house, he said. However, I loved it. It was unique, but Freddy didn't agree. He hated me so much that he ripped up my teddy, Jackson. My owner told me he would get a new one, so he went to the shops, but when he got home, Freddy escaped. It was too late. He was long gone.

Bobbie Brown (9)
Hilldene Primary School, Romford

Sycops And The Space Enemies

Sycops was in space exploring far and wide. Suddenly evil enemies came down destroying his world. They attacked his friends, Bloop, Blop and Blip. He heard a scream, "Help, help."
"Sid Sycops I'm coming to find you."
Sid Sycops saved his planet, Pluto. He had a celebration. He had lots of stuff... balloons, presents and cake. He loved it all and danced and played party games and singing. He played with his friends, Blip, Blop and Bloop.

Harvey-Jay James (7)
Hilldene Primary School, Romford

The Big Thief

My story begins with a creature called Sillyruby who has an enemy but it's not a bad enemy. They stole lots of stuff from Sillyruby and he's very mad after. He will go and catch the thief who got his stuff. Next, the bad guy was too fast and Sillyruby could not get the thief. After Sillyruby went back to his island, he ate food and it was good. Next, the thief came back and he had backup. Sillyruby came outside and he was mad, he was strong and got the thief.

Nicholas Ciobanu (9)

Hilldene Primary School, Romford

The Pet-Sitters

One day, Fluffy Mac Hairy was coming home from school (they called her Fluffy for short) and could hear barking, so she asked what was wrong.
The old lady said, "When I leave the house, I have no one to look after my pets."
That was when Fluffy had an idea to make a pet-sitter's club. She and the lady made the club and new members joined as they helped more people. Now, yetis from different planets and cloud planets let them pet-sit.

Zaya-Rose Bangali (10)
Hilldene Primary School, Romford

The Invisible Student

Once, there was an alien. He was a baby and then he fell through the sky. He was just a toddler and was sent to this thing called nursery. He was bullied for his ten eyes, eight hands and four legs. Then, he realised he could go invisible. He was getting back at the people who bullied him. Then, the teacher caught on, so they had a long talk about bullying. Since he was also royal, he banned bullying. One year later, he was the king of Alien World. He was great.

Misha Reece (10)
Hilldene Primary School, Romford

The Happy Ever After

Once upon a time, there was a monster called Angry Bob. He wanted to be on the Island of Calm, but he went to the Island of Angry and became annoyed. Angry Island had a number one enemy, the Island of Calm, but the Calm just wanted to help, so one day, they decided to go and help the Angry. When they arrived at the Island of Angry, they played calming music and did therapy and calming techniques to help them. They all became friends, and the Angry became Calm.

Sydney Eakers (11)
Hilldene Primary School, Romford

Spikos, The Best!

Spikos lived in Gibirislandia and one day, he found himself woken up by a very loud siren. Apparently, Godzilla - his biggest rival - had done an atomic breath in his town, so he got out of his underground bunker and went to save the day.
He got a nuke and did the unimaginable. He killed Godzilla! He was shocked and his city leader gave him the most lovely home ever!
He and his family were so happy. After all of that, they lived happily ever after.

Dennis Minaly (10)
Hilldene Primary School, Romford

The Secret Of The Dog, Ben

Once, there lived a ten-year-old dog called Ben. He was sweet in the day, but at night, he was the opposite of sweet. At night, he would crawl out of his bed and jump to open the door. If he looked at the moon, he would turn into a three-headed dog. He escaped and every night, he would eat any people left on the streets or when the moon was still out. Just in time for morning, he would head back to his home and when the sun came up he would be normal.

Sienna Rughoo (8)
Hilldene Primary School, Romford

Worry Monster

Sharpy was a worry monster and one day a girl bought him. That night the monster cuddled the girl and took care of her.

One night the monster made the mum and dad laugh as well but the dad hurt his back from the monster pushing him down the side of the bed. Sharpy was always there for her and he's been doing that for six years now. His appearance is colourful; he has sharp teeth and big eyes. You can mute him as he has a zip for his mouth.

Bethany Kelly Pipes (11)
Hilldene Primary School, Romford

What, Wot?

One day there was Green Jelly Wot. He had wobbly arms and an arch-enemy. His name was King Red Jelly Wot. Red Jelly Wot wanted to rule the universe, but Green Jelly Wot needed to stop him. Green Jelly Wot changed into the shape of a bottle.
He saw King Red Jelly Wot. He jumped out of the bottle, and said "The hero is here!"
Green Jelly Wot flew into the air and squished Red Jelly Wot. Now, all the Jelly Wots are safe.

Stanley O'Hanlon (9)
Hilldene Primary School, Romford

The Three-Pupil Pest!

Scrat, from Planet Nophalogian, snuck through Emily's window. Emily (who was on her bed) screamed and shuffled backwards, hitting the headboard.
She yelped, but Scrat instantly muffled the sound. Unmuffling her, she stared into his three-pupil eye. She didn't let a peep come out of her mouth, hoping this was all a dream. It wasn't!
Eventually, Scrat muttered, "Hello... Emily!"
Unresponsive, she ran downstairs and dragged her mum and dad into her room. But, when they came in, Scrat was absolutely nowhere to be found - even after they'd searched the place from the floor to the grey, dirty ceiling.

Imogen Winter (9)
Moorhill Primary School, Cannock

Atemma Yeti

Shooting rapidly down to Earth, Creature King was desperate to see his brothers. As the mechanical engine blasted neon-green lasers, bloody patches emerged all over his jigsaw body, which was as hard as a gold bar.

Landing on a farm, he started his hunt. Without warning, Mermaid Horn spotted Creature King. Trying to grab him, they failed each time.

Eventually, Creature King found his family members, who were chimpanzees. They remained silent. They saw their enemy!

King Creature rushed to his ship and shot back into space, leaving his devastated brothers behind.

Kyzee Morgan (10)
Moorhill Primary School, Cannock

Save Me

Once upon a time, there was a monster named Blip who lived with his friend called Hip. One day, Blip and Hip went into an abandoned house and saw a red button, so they pressed it and a portal opened!

Hip said that it was dangerous and went home. When Blip went inside, he realised that he was in the human world!

After running away from multiple humans, he screamed because he was stressed. Suddenly, a bunch of animals came rushing over to him.

After pushing the animals into the portal, it disappeared.

He knew who had done it: Zig!

Lacey Crockett (10)
Moorhill Primary School, Cannock

The Return Of Humans

Fire shooting down, the Difference was ready for another battle with the blood-belting humans. The Difference used their most valuable weapon: teeth. All of the sticky grass and dirt stuck to his teeth. Woo! Teeth went flying toward humans. The spacecraft fell to the ground.
"Look who's back!" said the Difference, with a smirk on his face. "I will use everything I've got." Unexpectedly, the humans started choking on a piece of metal, which magically appeared in their mouths, choking them until they dropped dead.

Ethan Russell (9)
Moorhill Primary School, Cannock

Eddie Makes Friends

Eddie loves to eat animals and people. He lives on Jupiter.

Eddie decided to go on an adventure to find some friends. He transformed into a robot and set off to Earth.

He searched for days and days.

Finally, after days of searching, he found a group of monsters on the corner of the street, crying.

Eddie (the kind person he was) helped them get food and warm clothes.

Eddie decided for them to be friends and he was transported into a robot again.

They lived happily ever after on the lovely, warm planet called Jupiter.

Elena Bullock (9)
Moorhill Primary School, Cannock

The Secret Slime Of The Devil's Bag

Swoosh! Slime Robber built a rocket and landed on Earth with a bang. He admired the planet.

He was seen as a normal human, so he walked into the richest bank in England. He turned into slime and went under the doors, unseen.

Confidently, he hacked the vault and slid all the money into a special bag. He had one million pounds. Magically, his bag turned to slime, made a rocket and blasted off!

After nineteen light years, he was home! He opened his vault, put the money inside and shut the door!

Louie Tyler (10)
Moorhill Primary School, Cannock

Monsters Are Bullies

One glorious sunny day, there was a monster all by himself, always getting bullied by the Queen of Hearts. The Queen of Hearts hated him because he was ugly and stinky. This was because he had a lot of fur. The Queen of Hearts was cruel to him because he had five eyeballs. The Queen made him physically sick and out came meatballs from his mouth. Saga (the monster) ran away from the Queen of Hearts to his house, but he did not see that the Queen of Hearts had followed him. She started to bully him harshly at home.

Evie-Rose Harley (9)
Moorhill Primary School, Cannock

World War Three

In a flash, Gentle Giant sprung into action, powering his most powerful weapon to use against his worst enemies - the devils.

Gentle Giant hated them, but suddenly the devils came to heaven to attack. Gentle Giant knew this day would come.

He never thought that he would get caught, but that day he was captured. They took him to hell and turned him into a red devil. He was fierce and angry.

He would miss being a gentle giant, but for now, he was forced into being a furious giant.

Jaiden Pearson (10)
Moorhill Primary School, Cannock

The Great Battle Was In Play

Suddenly, Laser Beam heard a thud. It was Fluffy; Fluffy was Laser Beam's worst enemy.
Without warning, he sprung into action! He charged up his lasers and was ready to battle Fluffy.
Fluff balls were darting past him, lasers were coming past them.
It was a good battle, but Fluffy was hurt and fell into a massive pile of lava.
Laser Beam won! He was happy as ever and even had a party.

Freddie O'Neil (10)
Moorhill Primary School, Cannock

A Friend

Gorb lived on Gorbworld. Unfortunately, all his family were taken away by humans. Then, one strange day, he made a friend. It was a human! On this day, Gorb was scared. However, this human comforted him. It was Gorb's turn to be taken away.

"Hey, you can stay with me!" exclaimed the human. As quick as a flash, this kind human disguised him. They are still friends to this day.

Darcie Marlow (10)
Moorhill Primary School, Cannock

My Friend Tiny!

Far away, in a forgotten galaxy is the planet called Monstervanila and there is a creature called Tiny Tim. He wants to rule Planet Earth but his enemies are human bots and rats. He travels through a compacted space shuttle. He prepares to face his worst nightmare, he is about to meet. Out of the space shuttle he uses a freeze trick he learnt by himself and freezes the creature to death.

Amelia Sayers (10)

Moorhill Primary School, Cannock

The War

Powering up his spacecraft, Tiny was ready for battle. Freddie was already shooting - it was brutal.

Tiny won.

Back at Freddie's home, Deacon was getting ready for war. He arrived and started to shoot... It was a long war but sadly Deacon lost and died, just like his brothers. When Tiny got home, everyone was cheering for him. They rewarded him with a gold medal.

Charlie Lakin (9)
Moorhill Primary School, Cannock

Jerry And His Adventures!

There once was a crazy creature called Jerry. Jerry lived in the jungle, he has always lived on his own. He's always wanted to have his very own roommate so he decided to go off into the jungle. First level one was stressful with monkeys, noisy, annoying, crazy monkeys, but he had enough courage to do that. Moving on to stage two, knowledge, the river had no way across but on the shore there were logs. Jerry made it. Now the final step is bravery.

"Spikes!" Jerry shouted, "How do I do it?"

He pushed and there she was, Jerry's very own roommate!

Caitlin Taylor (10)
St Anne's Catholic Primary School, Leyland

This Is My Planet!

Curly was crying in his room because he was lonely and sad that he had no friends. Then all of a sudden, his room shook.

He rushed out of his house and saw a massive portal from the planet Ping.

"Run - the Goof Balls are coming!" shouted Curly.

The Goof Balls started shrinking everyone and putting them in jars.

Curly had an idea to save everyone. He got his hula-hoop and started to hula, creating a tornado to sweep the enemy back to their planet.

Curly then turned everyone back to normal.

Everyone cheered, "We love you Curly!"

Emma Firth
St Anne's Catholic Primary School, Leyland

The Making Of Planet Earth

One dull and cold day, a mechanical alien called Roboti woke up to the swishing waves from the neighbouring water planet.

He said, "Why do I have to live on Mars, right next to that boring water planet?" He decided to go to his lab and send some amazingly giant asteroids to crash down into the water.

Fantastically, it worked, as the next morning when he awoke, flashes of green and yellow emerged from the blue waterscape and glared into his eyes, so he called the amazing planet Earth. He jettisoned down to Earth and began to explore the wonderful planet.

James Hopkins (9)
St Anne's Catholic Primary School, Leyland

The Disco Monster

In outer space, there was a mysterious monster called Disco. He was very colourful and had only one enemy, the Party Poopers. One day, Disco heard the loudest bang. It was fireworks. Disco loved fireworks, so he went to check it out. Disco went at the speed of light and when he arrived, the Party Poopers were already there. Disco, with his scary tentacles, scared the Party Poopers away. Everyone went silent. He made his way in. The music continued. Disco started to dance. The colourful lights shone on him and everyone started dancing. The mission was completed.

Max Burgess (9)
St Anne's Catholic Primary School, Leyland

YoungWriters® Est. 1991

The Bang Of Boline

Once there was a place called Boline and it was a rough planet. It was boring, raining diamonds like it does every day. There was a teenager who shone out to everyone and he was called Five Ears. Five Ears always dreamt of incredible things.

Five Ears didn't tell anyone about his power but one day he got to put it to the test. There was an asteroid and it was about to break Boline into pieces. He stopped it. No one could believe it. Even Wibble Wobble smiled and celebrated! Everyone was shocked as he'd never smiled before.

Kian Robinson
St Anne's Catholic Primary School, Leyland

Sugar Heart

Once upon a time, there was a creature called Sugar Heart. Her superpower was that she could make people fall in love with each other.
But there was this guy called Bitter Heart and he made people break up. They were enemies and they hated each other.
One day, Bitter Heart made a potion to make everyone hate each other. Sugar Heart changed the potion and made Bitter Heart fall in love with her.
Everyone was happy and they loved each other. They created a world full of joy, peace and love. It was a lovely world!

Emily Miskolczi (10)
St Anne's Catholic Primary School, Leyland

Gloopy's Escape

Gloopy sprints away from the evil aliens, he runs into the alleyway but it's a dead end. The aliens catch up and Gloopy melts and slips the evil aliens up. Gloopy takes the opportunity to run. He runs and runs and runs, he looks back and sees the aliens catching up. He turns a corner and spots a rocket ship, he runs towards it. He slides on the rocket ship and waves goodbye to the evil aliens with a smug look on his face.

A couple of months later, Gloopy arrived on his home planet with his family safe and sound.

Tia Price (9)
St Anne's Catholic Primary School, Leyland

A Story Of An Alien

Once there was an alien who lived on a planet called Pang. The alien's name was Ping Pong and he loved to play ping pong but he had no friends to play with. So he made a robot friend to play with and then made a teleporter to go to Earth. He accidentally sparked a virus that made everyone very ill and they were mean to Ping Ping and wanted to send him back. But then he found a cure to help them and he gave it to everyone that was ill and made them all better. He left Earth and everyone was safe!

Elliot Barnes (10)
St Anne's Catholic Primary School, Leyland

The Lost Coin

On Earth was a hidden coin which belonged to the Firelooreans long ago, but now Dr Doogenschmitz was after it. He was an evil genius from Earth. Cyclorn was after it too. He was the leader of Firefloor and needed the coin to save his homeland. As Cyclorn drew closer to the coin Dr Doogenschmitz shot down his spacecraft and crashed down to Earth. Cyclorn used his powerful eye laser to shoot down Dr Doogenschmitz's aircraft. He ran to the coin and retrieved it. His homeland was safe forever. Phew!

Sophie Moss (9)

St Anne's Catholic Primary School, Leyland

The Battle Of The Kingdoms

One morning, the King of Light was eating breakfast when his humble servant told him they were being ambushed by the Duke of Darkness. So the King announced through a microphone, "Everyone get to your battle stations."
The King himself went out to deal with the Duke of Darkness. So he brought the cursed Dual Katanas and the Duke of Darkness brought his Dark Blade. They both fought and fought, blow after blow until finally the King of Light had won and now he ruled over both kingdoms.

Kian Dickinson (10)
St Anne's Catholic Primary School, Leyland

Sparky And The Never-Ending War

Once upon a time, a crazy, giant, bright monster was saving the city from crashing meteors that rushed into the rough, aged concrete.

Eventually, it stopped, but he woke up to a strange voice in his head.

Several months later, he heard it again.

He was wondering, "Could this be the problem from the meteors?"

One day, he got up bravely and went to the largest trampoline in the world - ten thousand miles long - and jumped up to Star Venom and beat him up.

Noah Larkin (9)

St Anne's Catholic Primary School, Leyland

The Mystery

One dark, gloomy night, Luca was supposed to go to bed but he ignored his mum and snuck out of the house and ran away. His mum, Sandra, was worried about her son for so long and even started looking for him and she started crying saying, "Where is my son?"

She was trying to stop crying but she heard a scream. She ran over to the scream. She found out that it was her son and he was in big trouble. So he went back to bed and Luca was happy to be in his comfy bed again.

Daisy-Mae Ball (10)

St Anne's Catholic Primary School, Leyland

89

Izzy And Her New Friend

Izzy was in a new school so she wanted to make new friends but on her first day of school, she saw a person waving at her. But after being friends for one month, her friend betrayed her. Izzy felt so sad that she was off school for three days, but when she came back to school, she saw a note from a girl named Amy on her desk. Izzy was puzzled, but then she read the note. She ran up to Amy and hugged her. Izzy realised that Amy wanted to be her friend but she was too shy.

Nadia Matuszny (10)

St Anne's Catholic Primary School, Leyland

Earth's End

Jimmy the alien kept getting uninvited guests (humans) on his planet, so Jimmy decided he had to stop Earth. He made robotic machines, travelled to Earth and fought them.

They ended up losing thousands of aliens but ended up killing every country apart from America, which did better than all the other countries, but the robot lasers were able to kill them because they could shoot through walls. When they came home, they all drank their favourite drink.

Rory Winder (10)
St Anne's Catholic Primary School, Leyland

The Battle Of Doom

Once upon a time, Apophis, a dark demon, threatened people to take their precious Nile, the source of life. Horus, an air god, just became king but right when he became king... *Boom!* Something dark, mysterious was coming. "I shall rule the beauty of Egypt!" Horus exclaimed. Horus didn't know what he would see in front of his eyes. A dark, big hole was getting bigger. Everybody was petrified.

"Run for your lives!" they shouted in fear.

"What is this?" Horus said. He called Ra, the Sun god, to help. He agreed. Apophis was nearing the Nile, but they killed Apophis and saved the beautiful land. He never attacked again.

Daniel Fares (8)

The Batt CE Primary School, Witney

Fluffy The Unwanted Monster

Once there was a soft and friendly monster called 'Fluffy'. She wandered around on her own. She didn't like that but her friends didn't know that yet. A boy called 'Timmy' also walked around looking a bit shy. Fluffy sometimes walked past him and when Timmy looked at her slowly, he turned around, looking sad and gloomy.

Fluffy had always wanted to be friends with Timmy, so Fluffy walked towards him and said, "Hi, can we be friends?"

"Sure!"

"Woohoo! I knew I would find a friend someday," shouted Timmy.

"Thanks, BFF," replied Fluffy.

And together, they were friends.

Sophie Wakefield (8)
The Batt CE Primary School, Witney

Aliens On The Loose!

Once upon a time, there were people and a scientist who were waiting for some astronauts to come back from space.

Two weeks later, finally, the astronauts came back. Bad news, because when the astronauts were on the planet, the moon, aliens were following the astronauts secretly. But guess what? The astronauts didn't know what exactly happened on the journey. When the astronauts came back, it was the aliens against the USA. Now, the USA has lots of people but what the USA did not know was that half of the aliens were coming to the UK...

Ray Garbrah (7)
The Batt CE Primary School, Witney

Bob The Friendly Monster Visits Earth

Bob came from Planet Zing to Earth, to spy on humans. He wasn't a bad monster, he was just curious about what humans were and what they did. He was able to turn himself invisible to sneak around and spy. However, his invisibility power wore off and a boy called Edward saw him! Edward was a friendly boy who wanted a friend to play with and asked Bob to play with him. They played all day and night with Edward's toys and had the best time. Bob had to go back home but said one day he would definitely visit Edward again.

Zach Wyatt (8)
The Batt CE Primary School, Witney

The Disappearance Of Rubgrub!

Long ago, there was Rubgrub, a weird and wonderful creature. He had a special rainbow cloud that gave him air. But one day, Rubgrub was kidnapped by John, his enemy and he was trapped in a metal cage. One month later, in the middle of the night, Rubgrub saw a light. It was Queeny! Rubgrub's crush. She had come to save him but with an axe! So Queeny killed John and opened the cage. When they got back, Rubgrub and Queeny were married and the wedding was beautiful. Now they have got children, Jane and Jojo.

Livvi Green (8)
The Batt CE Primary School, Witney

The Water Creature

A little girl was by the water and she saw a blue light. She was so scared, she told her mum. They got into the car as fast as they could. Then, the three-eyed mermaid, Lola, jumped out of the sea and everyone was frightened. The whole town turned into a massive giant. A random person went into the sea and turned into a giant Kraken, kicking Lola far, far away, never to be seen again. The town clapped for the random person. The town was really happy that they were safe.

Mollie Armson (8)
The Batt CE Primary School, Witney

John And The Bully

"Aah!" screamed John as Goblino and Lala chased him. "Stop it," he had never screamed so loud before in his life.

"We're not gonna stop," Goblino said scarily.

"Goo goo gaa gaa," Lala gibberished.

"Oh!" said John as he fell.

"We've got you now John," said Goblino.

"Ha ha hee hee," laughed Lala.

"Hello," said Bartholomew, the teacher.

"I'm gonna beat you."

"What are you doing?" said Bartholomew.

"Nothing," said Goblino suspiciously.

"Well you have to be doing something," said Bartholomew.

"Goo goo ga ga," said Lala.

"Shut up," said Bartholomew.

"Okay, I was beating up John."

Principal, "No, wah!"

Jasper Clarke (10)
Waringstown Primary School, Waringstown

Nugget Vs Mr Pasta

Boom! "What was that crash?" We landed on Earth. "Mr Pasta is here."

"Let's go stop him before he destroys the Earth. There he is! Nugget, let's hide and see what he does."

"Haha! Look at me! I'm setting everything on fire! Woo hoo!"

"Okay, Nugget, go grab the matches off his spaceship."

"Okay, I'll do it."

Sneeze. "Aah! I banged my foot!"

"Hey, who's there?"

Gasps. Nugget pulls out a gun.

"Come on, Nugget!" I scream.

"Haha, *run!*"

"Okay, I think we are safe, okay." Nugget shoots Mr Pasta.

"*Yes!* Nugget, good job, woohoo."

Penny Hanna (10)
Waringstown Primary School, Waringstown

99

Chubble And The Sheep-Squisher

Chubble looked at the dead sheep. He'd just flown in from Planet Meyes.

Who'd leave a sheep here? he wondered.

From nowhere appeared Little Bo-Peep, waving her crook and yelling, "You monster, you sheep-squisher!"

Although Chubble didn't like sheep, he'd meant no harm, but Bo-Peep's angry tirade silenced him.

Suddenly, a van pulled up. Two men hopped out.

"All right, Peeps," said one, with a knowing wink.

"Here's the usual tenner," he said, passing her the money.

He gathered up the sheep, tossed it into the back of the van, slammed the doors shut and drove off. Bo-Peep went quiet and blushed.

Alexander Buchanan (10)

Waringstown Primary School, Waringstown

Drowning Out The Bully

On Planet Furry Feet live lots of different monsters. The young monsters are scared because Brenda Bully is making their lives miserable.

Brenda is tall and very hairy. She is calling other monsters names like 'Big Eyes', 'Slowcoach' and 'Baldy Feet'. The younger monsters feel very small and wish they were different.

Courageous Claire is walking past and hears Brenda's nasty words. Claire goes up to the younger monsters and blows confidence bubbles into their ears.

Immediately, the monsters start to encourage each other, saying, "You're cool, funny and pretty." They realise their compliments drown out Brenda Bully.

Maisie Harrison (10)
Waringstown Primary School, Waringstown

101

Techron's Cosmic Café

Once upon a time, there lived a space snake called Techron who loved to eat stars. Techron had been travelling around the galaxies for light-years, nibbling and gobbling up the prettiest and brightest stars, as they were the tastiest. Growing longer with each star-shaped snack, Techron was almost intergalactic in length! As Techron entered his next cosmic café, he was greeted by its protector, Electrospike. Electrospike attacked Techron. Sparks flew and his stars were scattered into Electrospike's galaxy. It was now the brightest of all the cosmic realms! Techron slithered away, only half his original size, ready to begin once again.

Joshua Hutchinson (10)
Waringstown Primary School, Waringstown

Goober's Goo Party

As a baby, Goober looked like every other baby. But as he grew, he looked more like a monster. When good things happened Goober would ruin them by spraying everything in green, sticky goo from his hands.

At his classmate's birthday, Goober sprayed everyone with goo when the cake arrived. The parents were cross.

"I don't belong here. I'm different," said Goober, sadly.

Goober went to live with other monsters on Planet Goo.

Goober's classmates missed him, so they threw a goo party to show Goober that being different made him special. Goober was delighted.

"This is where I belong."

Phoebe Armstrong (8)
Waringstown Primary School, Waringstown

The Mischievous Monster

In a mystical forest, Me-Me Mushroom lived with his vibrant red skin and glowing green eyes. This little troublemaker loved playing pranks on unsuspecting creatures, like tickling squirrels and making birds sing silly songs. But underneath its mischievous nature, Me-Me Mushroom longed for companionship.

One day, a brave little fairy called Lily crossed paths with Me-Me. She saw beyond the monster's tricks and recognised its kind heart. Together they formed an unbreakable bond, spreading laughter and joy throughout the enchanted forest and magical fair woods. The two friends were inseparable. They both lived happily ever after!

Ella Bushe (10)
Waringstown Primary School, Waringstown

Dragagift And The Monster Drones

Dragagift is in the illusions created by the Monster Drones trying to take over and destroy Planet Eternity.

Dragagift used his electric breath to electrocute them all, he said, "How am I going to spin this? Take cover!" he shouted to his gang. Dragagift absorbs more energy from electricity to become more powerful. His anger increased which caused him to implode. The Monster Drones were overwhelmed by the power and they all shut down. The illusion was broken and peace was restored to Planet Eternity.

Dragagift and his gang returned and were celebrated as heroes! *Teamwork makes the dream work!* Done!

Aimee May Freeburn (9)
Waringstown Primary School, Waringstown

Lovely Lucy Vs Angry Alfie

Lovely Lucy was an alien. She lived in a town called Emotion, inside of a girl called Emily. One day, she was with her friend Helpful Helen. A buzzer rang.

"We need Lovely Lucy," said a voice.

"Sorry, need to go!" she said, darting to Central Control. Lucy jumped on a plane and flew away to Brain.

"Ha ha!"

Lovely Lucy knew that voice. It was Angry Alfie. He was putting bad thoughts into Emily's head.

"Oh no!"

Lucy pulled out a slime gun and shot him in the bottom. He ran away, crying, "My bottom!"

Well done! thought Lovely Lucy.

Erin Peacocke (8)
Waringstown Primary School, Waringstown

Skills Can Save The World

A monster called Jigglebits lived in Monstermash. His friend was called Higgly Piggly. One day, they were practising gymnastics at the park, when suddenly, aliens appeared. This scared the monsters. Higgly even fainted. The aliens said they were going to take over Monstermash.

Jigglebits said, "I'll never let that happen! We have to show them we are brave and not afraid. Let's show our best gymnastics skills."

So the monsters did somersaults, aerials, cartwheels and backflips. The aliens knew they would never win this battle and quickly flew away. The monsters shouted, "We did it!"

Elise Liggett (9)
Waringstown Primary School, Waringstown

The Mythical Cards

Bob bobbed happily through Bobly Galaxy delighted with his pack of Griffin cards. These cards were not ordinary cards but held mythical creatures.

Suddenly, his enemies, Nob and Eob, jumped out.

"Hand over your Griffins!" shouted Nob.

Bob shape-shifted ahead, shouting, "Never!"

He threw a card to the ground. A Cyclops came to life from the card, sending Eob and Nob falling backwards.

Next, he threw out a card with monkeys. They started laughing and tickling them.

Bob put the cards in his pocket and walked off, shouting, "Looks like you both lost again!"

Edward Cassells (9)

Waringstown Primary School, Waringstown

T.U.Bs' Takeover!

Astounded, Luke watched as Ben acted unusually.
His sleepy eyes tightly shut and his fingers and
thumbs moved rapidly, like he was playing a
computer game. Beside him, Shirley sat, all sad,
emotional and grumpy. In the corner of his eye, he
spotted tiny, red-eyed, furry bugs flying around
them. T.U.Bs! Suddenly, they were everywhere,
coming out of technological devices and distorting
kids' brains. Yet this was unnoticed by the adults. It
was up to Luke to save them! Smarty Scientist
Luke invented a techno bug spray which made all
T.U.Bs shatter into pieces and made them kid-
friendly. Hooray!

Noah Budde (10)
Waringstown Primary School, Waringstown

Sensory City

A little girl was sitting in class. She was finding it very hard to focus on the day's lessons. She had ADHD and couldn't seem to settle herself. She made a wish for Soothing Suzy to come and help her to calm down.

In Sensory City, Soothing Suzy heard the little girl's wish. She said to herself, "That Befuddled Betty has been at her work again." Suzy gathered a couple of her sensory buddies - Happy Heidi and Focus Freda. They dashed off to the school, landing on the girl's desk quietly. The girl was delighted. She could now focus in class. Mission accomplished!

Tiffany Brown (8)

Waringstown Primary School, Waringstown

The Big Mistake!

It was a normal day in the lab and Elderbone was working on his shrinking potion with his friend, Colourful Clammy. Clammy knocked over the potion by mistake and spilt it all over Elderbone's wing which made it shrink! *Colourful Clammy will now be my arch-nemesis*, thought Elderbone. *Ugh, I just hate him now. Oh no, I can't fly anymore*, he thought. He tried and tried to fly but only managed to hover. *I need to get Colourful. Oh! I don't even want to say his name*, thought Elderbone. *I am one-winged. But... I will get revenge. Hahahahaha.*

Ella Owens (9)
Waringstown Primary School, Waringstown

Hairy Harry Gets One Over

It was a normal day on Planet Hirsute when Hairy Harry got out of his hammock. Unknown to Hairy Harry, Shaven Simon had plotted to shave all of Hairy Harry's beautiful, brown hair. Shaven Simon, armed with an electric trimmer, hid behind a palm street. A gloom of light reflected off Shaven Simon's bald head alerting Hairy Harry to Shaven Simon's sneaky plan. So he prepared to use his special hair-growing power. Quietly, Hairy Harry sneaked behind Shaven Simon and *kaboom!* Shaven Simon was covered, head to toe, in long, flowing, wavy, curly, shiny, silky blonde hair!

Ezra Gault (10)

Waringstown Primary School, Waringstown

Flying On A Myth

Joe was relaxing on the beach thinking about mythical creatures. He felt sleepy when he saw the biggest black shape fly across the sky. *Could it be? No, it couldn't. They're myths*, thought Joe. It was a dragon! It had hawk-like talons but most impressively, it could turn invisible. *I can't believe my eyes*, thought Joe. The dragon landed and approached Joe. It was offering to fly Joe up into the air. Joe got on and then felt the best thing in his entire life: flying on a myth. They soared through the clouds and then saw the whole glistening island below.

Isaac Wethers (9)
Waringstown Primary School, Waringstown

BSU KCITS

It was a sunny day on Planet Earth. All of a sudden, BSU KCITS appeared nastily on all the computer screens throughout the world and said, "Humans, you will give me all your data or else you will never be able to communicate with each other ever again!"

Suddenly, USB Stick appeared with his pet teddy. "Don't worry humans! I will help you. BSU KCITS is just a nasty virus. With my pet teddy's magic antennas, we will use the power of electricity to back up your data and remove the virus forever. BSU shouted, "No!"

"Yay! Yipee!"

Joshua Wylie (10)
Waringstown Primary School, Waringstown

Friendship

Once upon a time, there were two monsters called Oglaboogla and Chicken Wing, they were enemies. They went to the same job and every day they would fight until one day someone came in, it was Jimmy. He saw them fighting and he stopped the fight. "Why are you two fighting?" They were scared because Jimmy was the strongest man alive and he said again, "Why are you two fighting?" "One said, "Because he is an evil brat."

Jimmy said, "Why don't you get along? Go to the park."

They did and said, "This is so fun."

Harley Hughes (8)
Waringstown Primary School, Waringstown

Candy Cuddles To The Rescue

Evie was sitting in her bedroom, feeling upset and lonely. The girls in her class had not been very nice to her over the past week.

Suddenly, in Cuddlesville, Candy Cuddles' arms started to grow and vibrate. Someone needed a big cuddle! But who? Candy Cuddles activated her horns to fly and find out who was sad. They directed her to Evie's bedroom.

A few minutes later, Candy Cuddles was at Evie's, giving her a massive double-armed cuddle. She told Evie to ignore the nasty girls and that she would always be her friend. Evie smiled and felt happier.

Molly Lockhart (10)

Waringstown Primary School, Waringstown

The Loving Moon Sprite Luna

Let me tell you a story about a mystical creature called Luna the Moon Sprite. Luna had shimmering silver wings and a glowing aura that lit up the night sky. She would sprinkle stardust across the land, bringing dreams to life and filling hearts with magic. Luna's laughter sounded like twinkling stars and her presence brought a sense of peace to all who encountered her. People would look up at the moon and feel Luna's gentle touch, knowing that she was watching over them with love and kindness. Luna the Moon Sprite truly was a wondrous and enchanting creature.

Chloe Cunningham (10)
Waringstown Primary School, Waringstown

Teamwork!

On Planet H2O there was a ship sinking. Alarms rang out around all the galaxies. Many aliens lifted their heads but did nothing about it. But, on Planet Hydro, a young alien named Dewdrop begged her parents to let her go and help. Her parents gave in and she set off. As she headed down the aquatic path her friend Rosie came out and asked if she could come too. "Of course," said Dewdrop. When they reached the sinking ship they both dived under the water and sucked the water through the hull and mended it. Mission accomplished.

Elisabeth Smyth (10)
Waringstown Primary School, Waringstown

Naughty Nora Goes To The Moon

One day Naughty Nora was bored so she went to explore the moon without telling her mum or dad. When Naughty Nora arrived, she was bursting with excitement but all of a sudden Horrid Henry was there as well.

They both stared at each other but Nora said to herself, "It's okay." So she went over to her enemy and pushed Horrid Henry off the moon without even fighting.

Nora said, "That was fast to get over with." When it was over she started to get really sleepy and tired so she went back home to Neptune and went to sleep. Job done.

Dinah Glendinning (9)
Waringstown Primary School, Waringstown

War On Planet Zeb

It's a peaceful day on Planet Zeb when a massive ship crashes into the planet. Sturdy, Dizzy's enemy, leads his army off the ship. Sturdy wants to destroy Dizzy and take over his planet. Dizzy and Sturdy fall into a crater in the planet. They can't find a way out. They stop fighting each other when they become tired. Dizzy and Sturdy start talking and realise they might get out by cooperating. Dizzy and Sturdy make a ladder together to escape and tell their followers that helping each other is better than fighting, even though they are different in ways.

Adam Coffey (9)

Waringstown Primary School, Waringstown

Mission Possible

On Planet Footon, the hero Ronaltoes has been doing keepy-uppies to ensure the planet stays happy. He has been sent to Earth to find a replacement for the ageing hero and keep his arch-enemy, Klopptonite, from destroying the planet's sole. After many trials, a new hero has been found that can do the most keepy-uppies and his name is Fernantoes. Ronaltoes and Fernantoes return to the Planet of Dreams, but when they arrive they discover that Klopptonite has turned the planet into a nightmare and will never ever win anything again due to Klopptonite's boys.

Noah Chestnutt (10)
Waringstown Primary School, Waringstown

Messi The Monster

Messi was a skilled footballer monster. He has a hard football head and four different feet with different skills to help him carry out his missions. His two hands help him be invisible when he puts his hands together. He goes on fire when he sends out red cards. Messi was sent on a long mission to take over another monster creature, Ronaldo. He was short, hairy and thought he was clever. In the final mission, Messi used his skills to stop Ronaldo from trying to take his power. Messi went invisible, passed Ronaldo and headed the ball into the top bins. Hooray!

Micah Parks (9)

Waringstown Primary School, Waringstown

The Homework Gnasher

One day, a scientist was trying to invent a plant to help children with their homework. In the lab, he accidentally spilt the wrong potion on the seedling and it began to grow and transform into a monster plant with an appetite for homework books.

The monster escaped the lab and went on the hunt for homework books. It spent the rest of its life travelling the world, devouring homework and annoying teachers.

School children loved the creature because it got them out of doing homework, but teachers are constantly trying to track it down and stop it.

Jake Robinson (9)
Waringstown Primary School, Waringstown

Snowy Scares

Snowy was a very clever yeti who attended Yeti Academy. He was very lonely as he wasn't like the other yetis because he didn't like scaring people. On the day of the scaring competition, Snowy was really nervous, but when his turn came, he went up to the scare monitor. Snowy thought roaring was like shouting and he always got told off for shouting, so he lifted his arms, pulled the scariest face and said a little 'boo'. The scare monitor exploded because everybody had a big roar, but no one pulled a scary face. Snowy won! Everybody cheered.

Noah McIlwaine (9)
Waringstown Primary School, Waringstown

Miss Wiggly Saves The Day

A girl called Evie lived in Crinkly Bottom. She was sad because she had lost her favourite doll Georgia. Evie made posters to find Georgia and put them up in town. She got upset looking at the posters. Along came Miss Straight and Miss Wiggly. Miss Straight was always very serious and told Evie she needed to be careful with her belongings. This upset Evie even more. Miss Wiggly did her silly wiggle dance to cheer Evie up. When Evie calmed down, she remembered leaving Georgia in the park. Miss Wiggly and Evie wiggled their way to the park and found Georgia.

Aimee McCullough (8)
Waringstown Primary School, Waringstown

Zoe's Big Adventure

Once upon a time, there was a mer-dragon called Zoe. Her home planet Nep-Tune was known for being perfect.

However, Zoe wanted something more from life, so she decided to take her mermaid tail and dragon wings and fly to Earth.

She was happy she was on Earth, but something was missing. She left her best friend, Meredith, on Nep-Tune.

So she flew back to Nep-Tune to get her, so that she could experience the craziness and wonder. While they loved their time on Earth, they decided it was time to go home to Nep-Tune and tell their friends.

Lucy Ball (9)
Waringstown Primary School, Waringstown

The Story Of Good And Bad

Kute Keven was having his healthy lunch of fish when he noticed Bully Boris the ice griffin fly past his window on a mission to cause chaos and disappointment at Central Park Ice Rink. Kute Keven realised that Bully Boris was planning to melt the ice so the kids couldn't skate and have fun. Kute Keven followed Boris to stop him but when the kids saw Kute Keven they didn't want to skate. They wanted Kute Keven to give them a ride on his back around the park. Bully Boris' plan had backfired spectacularly. Kute Keven's mission was complete.

Noah McAdam (9)
Waringstown Primary School, Waringstown

Wriggle's Adventure

The alarm went and Wriggle rushed to the door alongside his cousin Giggle. The competition was on! Who would get to the little girl first? Wriggle dashed into his rocket. He was saying goodbye to Planet Rescue. It was a race for time. Both Wriggle and Giggle landed on Earth at the same time but then stopped running and looked at each other. They realised that they shouldn't be racing each other and that they should be working together to save the little girl. When they realised what they were doing wrong they saved the little girl! Job well done!

Amelia Armstrong (10)
Waringstown Primary School, Waringstown

The Gold Medallist

Doctor Webbugger is in his office and he is very excited because today he will be competing in the Olympics! Doctor Webbugger is aiming to win a gold medal in backflips. Doctor Webbugger needs to do 150 backflips in less than one minute to win the gold. He has a snack of peony roses and rhubarb, which is his favourite lunch and he grows them at his house in Plant Land. Doctor Webbugger completes 150 backflips in fifty-eight seconds, setting a new world record. He takes his gold medal back to his office to finish his day's work! Olympic Champion!

Ben Whittaker (9)
Waringstown Primary School, Waringstown

Seek's Revenge

My crazy creature is called Seek; he is Spanish. Seek is from the Canary Islands, and he is able to do loads of tricks when playing football. His favourite trick is doing rainbow flicks. Seek has one enemy, King Kong; they really hate each other! They were talking one day when Seek said something that King Kong didn't like, so King Kong kicked Seek. Seek got King Kong back by doing a football tackle on him; he two-footed King Kong, which broke his leg! King Kong went to hospital because of this and wasn't allowed home for two months.

Alfie Davidson (8)
Waringstown Primary School, Waringstown

What A Lie!

My friend Susie and I were camping in the forest. Sitting by the campfire planning our adventure, we heard a loud noise and were horrified at what we saw. This horrible creature said she was Crazy Lizzie from Planet Bonkers and she could see into the future; that made her many enemies. She yelled that before morning she would turn us into mini monsters and then disappeared. Susie and I sat up all night worrying what the morning would bring. Too worried to sleep, it was a long night but morning came at last and what a relief! We were unchanged.

Emily Derby (9)
Waringstown Primary School, Waringstown

The Lost Alien

Once, an alien called Bob was flying his ship when it broke down! Bob landed on a planet called Earth. He found strange creatures called humans. "I can't let them see me, they'll freak out!" he said. Bob figured out he couldn't turn invisible or teleport anymore. Bob realised he needed a new engine for his ship so he could get back home! He found a car shop and sneaked with his tentacles an engine and ran away before the shopkeepers noticed.

He quickly installed the engine on his ship and flew away to his home!

Lucas Thompson (10)

Waringstown Primary School, Waringstown

How Supagriffgon Saved The Day!

The Griffin Dragon is a hero. She saves people and helps other living things.

One day, Supagriffgon was flying over Earth, going to Kristy the monster's birthday party, when she heard screaming from below. Lots of people were screaming, "Help!" So she went down like a meteor. Saving the whole world was hard, but she went down to fight that big monster called Mr Naughty. He was very slimy but she went down to take him down. She was very focused on getting him down and she did. She saved the world once again. She was a hero.

Lily-Anna Hutchinson (9)

Waringstown Primary School, Waringstown

Extra Emmie Saves The World

Once upon a time, there was Turbo Turtle who wanted all humans destroyed. He lived on Pluto with other monsters, no one liked Turbo Turtle because he would always laugh at private jokes. So Turbo Turtle decided to throw an asteroid at Earth but Extra Emmie stopped the asteroid at the last second. Extra Emmie decided to build a time machine and set the time machine to 928 AC and punched Turbo Turtle into the time machine to teach him a lesson. Extra Emmie broke the time machine so that Turbo Turtle couldn't come back, the world was saved!

Clara Little (9)
Waringstown Primary School, Waringstown

Gobleycook's Adventure

A monster named Gobleycook was fluffy and he could breathe in space.

One day Gobleycook was floating in space, but then, space had a space shake and he fell down to Earth. Everyone looked at him in disgust and Gobleycook was sad, but one girl did not and her name was Ella. Ella came over and gave him a hug and he was happy. Ella and Gobleycook became best friends. Gobleycook couldn't stay on Earth for long. He asked Ella's mum if Ella could get into a spacesuit and go into space. She said yes. Gobleycook and Ella were happy.

Sophie Bailey (8)

Waringstown Primary School, Waringstown

Jackasoures

Jackasoures was from Yoshi's Island. His best friend was Isaac. They liked to get up to all sorts of mischief together, especially in school. Their teacher was Mr Brown. They liked to pull pranks on him in class. Once, they left a whoopie cushion under his seat. The whole class laughed when he sat on it and it made a silly noise. Mr Brown tried his best to keep a straight face and shouted, "Who put this here?" Jackasoures and Isaac owned up to placing it under his seat. Mr Brown gave them school rules to write out ten times.

Isaac White (10)

Waringstown Primary School, Waringstown

The Lifeguard

Eyewhal was a creature from a faraway land called Whaland. She now lived in the warm waters of a beautiful and busy beach. Eyewhal certainly looked a bit strange, but she was certainly an amazing lifeguard!

One day, she noticed a young girl struggling to keep her head above the water. Eyewhal frantically swam over to help her. Eyewhal heroically saved the girl with her incredible horn by thrusting her up above the surface of the water so that she could finally fill her lungs with air again. The lifeguard had definitely done her job!

Jessica Riddle (9)
Waringstown Primary School, Waringstown

Michael The Superhero

One sunny day, Michael was flying around. Down below, he saw a cat stuck in a tree.

Meow! Meow! the cat cried.

"Oh no!" said Michael and he climbed up the tree to save the cat. The cat smiled at Michael and went back home.

Michael zoomed away to see who else needed his help. While he was running, he saw a robber trying to rob a store. When he saw this, he sprinted into action and knocked him out. Michael called the police with his phone and they arrested him. Michael was now tired and flew home to rest.

Scarlett Thompson (8)
Waringstown Primary School, Waringstown

The Alien Who Could Hunt On A Horse!

Beep! Beep! Beep! An alarm sounded in the Alien Station. Bob rushed to the phone.

"Hello," said a worried man. "I've got a fox on my farm." The man pleaded with Bob to sort it out. But Bob didn't have a horse. Bob flew down to Planet Earth, stole a horse from a random person's field, which he named Bob Jr and got a disguise for himself. He rode Bob Jr out to where the farmer had a fox problem. Bob and Bob Jr galloped across every field the farmer owned and chased every fox on the land away.

Poppy Thompson (10)
Waringstown Primary School, Waringstown

Planet Love

On Earth, a little girl was worried and scared on Planet Love. "Send me, please," said Cokeanbannaxxhappy. So they sent him, but at the same time, his enemy arrived. They both rushed to try and get there first. Hopefully, Cokeanbannaxxhappy gets there first. Then a fight happens, but Cokeanbannaxxhappy gets out of the fight first and rushes to Planet Love. Once he arrives he finds the girl and gives her a hug that chases all the worries away and leaves confidence, braveness and love in her head to go wherever she wants to go.

Jamie Thornbury (9)
Waringstown Primary School, Waringstown

Mars Versus Venus

Mars versus Venus, the planet World Cup Final! The score is 1-1 in the 80th minute. On the bench as always sits Jimmy Bob. Never gets a game. Always ignored. The manager looks around in desperation, spies Jimmy Bob. "Warm up!" he shouts to him. He can't believe it! 89th minute on he goes in time for a corner kick. In whips the ball, Jimmy Bob leaps into the air and heads it into the net. Goal! 2-1! Final whistle blows. They have won, all thanks to Jimmy Bob. He's a hero. Never on the bench again! Never ignored again!

William Massey (10)
Waringstown Primary School, Waringstown

Battle For The Earth

Once, there was Good and Bad. They didn't like each other, so they went to war. Good won so they got three-quarters of the Earth. Bad wouldn't give up, then became the species of Ookie, the most powerful monsters.

Ten years later a boy called Fang was born. He was raised to kill but he never grasped it. A war was about to begin. So he had to go without knowing what to do. He slaughtered everyone with his ingenious ideas but this fight was for the entire world. He killed 1008 but they shared the Earth and called a truce.

Josiah Martin (10)

Waringstown Primary School, Waringstown

Dotty's Race

It all started with a nice monster called Dotty. Dotty was from Planet Super; Dotty had an enemy called John who was from Planet Feet. There was a race to see who could run as fast as a human. They decided to play a game called Super Fast. John was losing, so he played tricks on Dotty, like splatting balloons on Dotty and changing the directions to go. *I don't like being tricked*, thought Dotty, so she managed to run past Super John. This made Super John cross and he got caught in one of his own tricks. *Nooo.*

Maisie Adair (9)
Waringstown Primary School, Waringstown

Stinky Pants Steve

Once there was a boy called Steve, he was playing outside and got mucky so he went inside to wash his clothes. His washing machine wasn't working and as he only had one pair of clothes he took them off and for weeks didn't wash. His pants started to stink. One day he went for a walk and saw his friends, Wash Cloth Wendy and Super Soapy Sophie. They didn't like that his pants were stinky, so they ran after him to try and wash him clean. They couldn't catch him so shouted after him, calling him Stinky Pants Steve!

Luke Hunter (9)
Waringstown Primary School, Waringstown

The Scare Of Blobly

Once there was a monster called Blobly and he lived in a world called Crazy King World. One rainy day, he got a message so he went down to Earth where he liked to scare children. So that's what he did.

He saw a child and thought, *This is the child.*

The child couldn't see him, so he crept up behind the child and he scared the child with his mind. Blobly made a crazy, scary image and pushed it into the child's head. He scared the child and wanted to scare more and so he did.

Then he went home.

Leah Parker (9)
Waringstown Primary School, Waringstown

Blobbing Along

One day, Blobbers was looking down at Earth from his planet, Mars. Blobbers noticed there was lots of litter. Blobbers hated litter! Blobbers got into his alien friend's UFO. He got to Earth safely and started lifting litter. It started sticking to him, so he snuck into someone's house and took a shower! Soon, he realised that he was in a sewer. He had melted down the drain! He ended up drifting down the sewer and he ended up in a park. He was scared, so he went back to Mars, but realised there was a girl in his tummy!

Esme Magowan-Wilton (9)
Waringstown Primary School, Waringstown

The Monster That Lived On Earth

From deep space in the year 2000, a strange creature crashed on Erath from his home planet called Alien-land, as he was trying to escape from his evil twin, Lizario. Lizario was jealous as Lizarazu was much better at juggling than he was and this made him upset and he wanted to chase him out of Alien-land. When Lizarazu crashed on Earth, he flew to the nearest city and was hiding at a circus where the ringmaster found him juggling behind the tent, so he gave him a part in the show as he was so good. The spectators loved him.

Brandon Elliott (9)
Waringstown Primary School, Waringstown

Super Zingo

In one corner of this land lived Super Ziza. In another corner of this land lived Mango Dango. One day, Mango Dango went to the mayor of Happyville and tried to kill him so he could rule. However, Super Ziza came to Happyville and looked around for a while until he found him. He got his brain metre and made Mango Dango's brain happy. Mango Dango was no longer evil and didn't want to rule Happyville anymore. In fact, he gave the mayor one million pounds and invited him to his house for a five-course meal.

Daniel Hamill (10)
Waringstown Primary School, Waringstown

The Land Of Sprinkles

In a land called Sprinkles, there was a boy called Gerry. He loved ice cream so much that he started a society to steal ice cream.

One day, the ice cream police saw him stealing ice cream. Gerry saw that they saw him. Gerry ran as fast as his little legs could take him. He was so, so, so scared. He got on a boat but the police didn't stop.

The boat took him to Waringstown Primary School. He pretended to be a student there who had just transferred to the school. The ice cream police never ever saw him again!

Annie McCallum (10)
Waringstown Primary School, Waringstown

Money-Maker Mike Makes Pounds From Pennies!

Mum was searching around the house for some money. She sighed with relief when she found a pound coin. She asked Harry to go to the shop to buy some milk.

Harry dragged his feet to the shop. Penniless Peter saw Harry and told him he would have some leftover money for sweets! Harry was tempted. Money-Maker Mike heard this and knew that Mum would be cross. Money-Maker Mike reminded Harry that it is important to save money for things that are needed. He taught everyone that if you save pennies then you can make pounds.

James Grant (9)
Waringstown Primary School, Waringstown

The Crazy Friday

A boy was frustrated on Earth. He was in the middle of his Friday test. He knew none of the answers. None! He decided to call Betsy the Brain for help.

She arrived and tried to help him. She had done all she could when Ryan Runner came along to help. He said, "Come with me," but the boy refused to.

Ryan Runner was called Ryan Runner because he was faster than anyone in the world at running. He took himself and started chasing after the poor boy. Thankfully, Betsy the Brain managed to stop him.

Nina Kraicova (9)
Waringstown Primary School, Waringstown

151

Planet Cray-Cray And Earth

There are two aliens, Fred and Frank, they are
enemies. Frank can be invisible by a push of a
button and has five eyes. Fred has three eyes and
a big mouth. The aliens were fighting when
suddenly the door opened and they fell off the ship
and landed on Earth.

A girl called Amelia found them and brought them
home. She noticed that they looked funny. She told
them she was an alien from Planet Cray-Cray.
Frank and Fred exclaimed that so were they and
they all went back to their families and home to
Planet Cray-Cray.

Eva Morrow (10)

Waringstown Primary School, Waringstown

Bob's Big Problem

Once upon a time, there was a spider. His name was Bob. Bob has long, super stretchy legs! He is blue and smooth with blood-red eyes. He was wandering around his home in the sewer when he heard loud yells. Bob wasn't sure if he should investigate. He didn't know who was yelling. The noise was from up above, but who was it? Bob crept slowly towards the gully. The yelling got louder and louder. Bob decided to use his stretchy legs to swing out and scare the noisy child away. Bob was able to relax now and sleep.

Archie McCullough (9)
Waringstown Primary School, Waringstown

Blue Bomber

Outer Neptune is usually a very happy place. Everybody lives in blue bubbles. Then, along comes the Green Goblin, who wants to make Outer Neptune green with his green mist. It's now up to the Blue Bomber to save Outer Neptune. First, the Blue Bomber has to find the Green Goblin. It is very easy. He just needs to follow the green mist.

When the Blue Bomber finds the Green Goblin, he gets his big hoover and sucks him and the green mist up.

The Blue Bomber saves the day and Outer Neptune is happy again.

Rhys Burns (10)

Waringstown Primary School, Waringstown

Rise Of The Troll

Once upon a time, there was a troll named Clobber.

Clobber's hometown was taken over by gremlins. All the trolls wanted to get their town back, so they mined and collected iron for ages until they made enough for everyone to get armour and shields etc. Then they went to the trolls' kingdom to get ready for battle.

The battle proved challenging, but not for Clobber who used his secret sword to defeat the gremlin king and win their hometown back. The trolls were happy and lived happily ever after.

Oliver Wright (10)
Waringstown Primary School, Waringstown

Stretch-No-Strong!

Bobby was on Mars for his holiday. He travelled to Mars using his super-stretchy arms. When it was time to go home, he noticed that his super-stretchy arms had jammed. He could not get back home to his fellow one-eyed creatures. After a long time of thinking and some stargazing, Bobby had a plan. Bobby made a spaceship out of rock. He used the oil from his leaking broken arms and his laser eye to set the red rock alight. When he saw the flame, he jumped on the spaceship and shot back to the moon and his friends.

Zachary McGrath (9)
Waringstown Primary School, Waringstown

Jeff And The Lost Coins

One day a monster called Jeff went to Planet Zong. He was meeting his friend Fred. Fred was his best friend and they were going to do a mission. They had to find gold coins that had been lost for a long time so they set off for an adventure.

When they got to Planet Zong they started to sing. Mrs Burr was very rude to them. "Go away!" Mrs Burr shouted and they thought that Mrs Burr was suspicious so they went to her house and found all the gold coins. They hi-fived and that was the mission.

Jacob Irwin (10)

Waringstown Primary School, Waringstown

Lexi's Adventure

One day, Lexi the fox went out on a stroll up her favourite mountain. Usually, she would meet her friend Olivia, the hummingbird, on her way up the mountain, but she didn't see her. So, she kept on walking up the mountain until she came to Olivia's perch and she didn't see her all curled up. So, she just carried on until she got to the top of the mountain and then she saw Olivia singing to all the forest animals. Lexi joined in with her and everyone was very happy singing along to the music!

Sarah Fitzpatrick (10)
Waringstown Primary School, Waringstown

Friends Forever Helping Lost Creatures' Souls

One day, when I was just a wolf cub playing with my siblings, hunters came. Mum quietly called us over. I saw a butterfly and followed it while my siblings went to our mother. A man-hunter picked me up and sold me to a circus. They beat me a lot and they beat my friend, Aries. We became spirits and helped others like us. Aries came to tell me that an elephant was lost, so I ran there. We helped her find her way back and she said we'd never be lost again... but now we're lost in the black abyss.

Alexandra Emo (10)

Waringstown Primary School, Waringstown

Me And My Monster

One night I heard banging noises from underneath the stairs. I was scared to look but I did it anyway. I screamed loudly because I saw a monster. I closed the door and ran away. A few days later I went back and we became friends. His name is Sloppy, he was sad because he lost his juggling balls. We went on an adventure to look for the balls and found them hiding behind the hall table. Sloppy was so happy. He taught me how to juggle. We had so much fun juggling together we stayed best friends forever.

Amber Dawson (8)
Waringstown Primary School, Waringstown

Dylan The Dynamite

Once upon a time, there was a creature called Dylan. He lived in a cave with his family. Dylan was born with a superpower that turned him into anything. One day, there was a storm that caused the cave to collapse. Dylan was trapped in the cave with his family. They tried to dig their way out but failed then Dylan remembered he could turn into anything. So he turned into dynamite to save his family, but he didn't make it out alive. Ever since he has been known as Dylan the Dynamite.

Dawid Pawlowski (10)
Waringstown Primary School, Waringstown

YoungWriters®
— Est. 1991 —

The Lonely Five-Eyed Monster

Mr Gary is really, really mean to his enemies but sometimes nice to others. He has five googly eyes and looks a little bit scary. Sometimes he gets lonely because of how he looks, he is not a very approachable monster and doesn't have very many other monster friends.

Mr Gary lives in the Giants Causeway. He loves it here as he has many rocks to hide behind. His stretchy arms help him move from rock to rock when he scares visitors who come near his home. Job done.

Kayla Brooks (9)

Waringstown Primary School, Waringstown

Gooey And Amber!

On Earth, there was a girl called Amber. She was sad and unhappy all the time. Then an alien from Planet One Eye came. His mission was to make Amber happy and cheerful, so Gooey flew down to Earth. Gooey said to Amber, "Hello! This is my first time being on Earth!" He spoke in a weird voice. Amber found it cool, so Amber and Gooey went to fun activities such as going to the park. Amber finally smiled after days and days of being sad. Gooey's mission was finally done.

Blake Cooper (10)
Waringstown Primary School, Waringstown

When Emily Found Bear

One morning, Emily got ready to go for a hike when she got up. She hiked through the forest and was surprised to find a three-legged horse. She named the horse Bear because she was big and cuddly. She looked around and found a rope she could use to bring Bear home to keep her safe. Bear dug a big hole in Emily's field and the next morning Emily woke to find that Bear had found buried treasure in the field.
Emily hugged Bear and they were best friends forever.

Lauren Orr (8)
Waringstown Primary School, Waringstown

Big Boy Bill

There he was, Big Boy Bill, sitting down on his chair. Then suddenly, he got an alert that someone was in danger. They were at Belfast Zoo and a lion had broken out of its cage. Big Boy Bill flew over there and when he got there, he saw the boy. He went over and turned into a piece of meat, but when the lion went to bite into him, he turned into a rock and broke the lion's teeth. Once again, Big Boy Bill saves the day!

Thomas Alexander (10)
Waringstown Primary School, Waringstown

Grego's Love

Once upon a time, Grego travelled to every planet to search for love. Having searched every planet, he still couldn't find love, so he came back to Venus, his home.

He walked in and to his delight, he found a beautiful dragon. She was called Grellia. She was very tall and pink. She had an amazing fur.

They fell in love at first sight and married. They had two children and they all lived happily ever after.

Konstancja Halaburda (10)
Waringstown Primary School, Waringstown

The Monster Who Is Always Happy

One day, Jimmy heard a siren, so he flew to the noise and saw a little girl, sad.
But before Jimmy could get to the girl, sadness stopped him.
So, he hit sadness and made the girl happy.
Job done.

Sebastian McAllister (9)
Waringstown Primary School, Waringstown

The Crazy Bird

In Jamaica, a bird was hurt, so Star came to the rescue then she got captured by a man. She was terrified.

The man was evil, mean and not kind.

Star was hurt but the man let her go.

Gracie-May Gore (9)
Waringstown Primary School, Waringstown

Stranded

Oliver's sailing on a yacht in the South China Sea when a big storm hits. This storm crushes the yacht into two. Reaching for a flare, the crew falls overboard leading to a painful perishing.

Oliver is left stranded on Nebarris Island. A cargo ship sails in. Three men climb out and knock Oliver unconscious with a stick. He wakes up in a cell below deck and is held for ransom.

For him to gain his freedom, he must defeat 'The Bone Crusher'. Oliver sees a vial labelled 'Mirrorquroo'. He chugs it. Now he is on his way to fight The Bone Crusher.

Ben Harris (10)
Woolton Primary School, Woolton

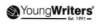

The Change!

Squg was sitting in school like he always did on a Monday morning when suddenly he felt a strange feeling he had never felt before. He put his hand up to go to the toilet. He rushed through the halls and slid into the toilets.

What is happening to me? he thought. All of his hair started to fall off. Human hands and legs grew. Squg screamed so loud that the teacher burst in and stood shocked with her mouth wide open. Squg had turned into a human!

The teacher screamed, "How did you get here?"

"It is me, Squg," he said in panic.

Isla Blu Geraghty (11)
Woolton Primary School, Woolton

The Lonely Monster

The lonely monster crawled out of the rubble and swam all the way to Wales, where he found a girl called Mia. The monster's name was Guoby. Guoby caused mayhem all over town to get Mia's attention. She had had enough, she tried for weeks but couldn't do it. She had an idea. She would be naughty to grab his attention. Every time she did it pulled him closer and closer to her, until one day Mia caught his attention. They both started to cause bad things to happen together. One by one, buildings crumbled.

Then she woke up from her dream.

Grace Reid (11)
Woolton Primary School, Woolton

The Wind-Up Frog That Went Mama

Sitting in my seat I was thinking of what to make. Maybe a tank for Rose (my goldfish). Or something more alive? What about a frog that can talk? I loved frogs so I thought it was a great idea.

In my garage, I found some green rusty metal to make its base, a windup monkey which I could use the key to make it come alive and four rusty legs. Now I needed a voice box. The only thing available was my sister's old doll.

"Mama!" the frog screamed over and over again. I couldn't sleep that night...

Eben Price (11)
Woolton Primary School, Woolton

Evil Friends

Volcano was happy with his mum and dad, but one day everything changed. His friends came over to play and they were having fun until... *Kaboom!* A mysterious rock. Volcano's friends were evil. He ran and ran until he reached an aircraft. He hopped on and started the aircraft, then he flew in the air in a matter of seconds, but his evil friends could fly too. Volcano flew to Japan and landed. He went in a bunker to hide, but then..."Argh."
What happened is a mystery.

Bobbi-Mai Keating (10)
Woolton Primary School, Woolton

The Spotty Man

One day I was minding my own business when Timmy came to play. He took one look at me and ran crying. His mum came with him, he couldn't even look at me. When his mother looked at me she grabbed Timmy and ran! That was the last day I saw Timmy's scared eyes.

After that day I never went outside. I was alone. One day a woman was in my room and said to go with her. It was my best idea ever. She was an angel. She said I was perfect.

Beth Palmer (10)
Woolton Primary School, Woolton

Tick, Tick, Tick

It was all quiet in the dark, damp cave. All but a little sound, *tick, tick, tick*; a little fly. A fly couldn't do any harm, could it? It flew out to find its next victim. It landed on an old man and it sucked, sucked the life out. The man's face collapsed and crumpled until it was like a dry prune. It was all quiet in the dark, damp cave. All but a little sound, *tick, tick, tick...*

Yizhi Qi (10)
Woolton Primary School, Woolton

YoungWriters® Est. 1991

Yetizar

Lightening struck! The village shook. This mysterious creature charged. A girl screamed as she saw the yeti covered in orange fur with green horns and yellow teeth poking out - it carried bricks forging through with its red, sharp scorpion claws. *Stomp! Stomp! Stomp!* There was another one... Is the myth of Yetizar true? All went dark! Was this the end?

Ella Dyce (11)
Woolton Primary School, Woolton

YOUNG WRITERS INFORMATION

We hope you have enjoyed reading this book – and that you will continue to in the coming years.

If you're a young writer who enjoys reading and creative writing, or the parent of an enthusiastic poet or story writer, do visit our website **www.youngwriters.co.uk**. Here you will find free competitions, workshops and games, as well as recommended reads, a poetry glossary and our blog.

If you would like to order further copies of this book, or any of our other titles, then please give us a call or visit **www.youngwriters.co.uk**.

Young Writers
Remus House
Coltsfoot Drive
Peterborough
PE2 9BF
(01733) 890066
info@youngwriters.co.uk

Scan me to watch the Crazy Creatures video!

YoungWritersUK   **YoungWritersCW**

youngwriterscw   **youngwriterscw**